TO A FURRY
SPECIAL KID:

· · · · · · · · · · · ·

FROM:

· · · · · · · · · · · ·

and your pal
Mr. Bean

Editor: Tina Neidlein
Writer: Cat Hollyer
Illustrator: Mirna Stubbs
Designer: Scott Swanson

Printed by Trojan Press, Inc.
Kansas City, Missouri

MR. BEAN

THE RULE-BREAKING PUP
and the HOUSE FULL of
LOVE

Illustrated by **Mirna Stubbs**
Written by **Cat Hollyer**

Mr. Bean is a fluffy-white dog—
the **fluffiest** you will meet!

He's **itty** and **bitty** and **scrappy** and **cute**
and he'll do anything for a **treat.**

His home's here at **Ronald McDonald House** now,
but his life wasn't always this cushy.
He once was a **hole-digging, fence-scratching** pup,
and at times he could be a bit **pushy.**

He dug up the **dahlias** and dug up begonias
and dug his way under the gate.
Then he ran in the street! WHAT A TERRIBLE MESS!
He caused traffic and **made people late!**

Mr. Bean got in pretty big trouble that day—
a policewoman gave him a ticket.
And she said, "You seem nice, but this digging is not.
It's a habit, and you need to KICK IT!"

So he headed for **home** with his tail 'tween his legs,
and he pondered that **nasty citation.**
He felt **sad** being **bad,** making everyone **mad**...
Bean just needed a **good occupation!**

Best
garden
award

So he put on his **spiffiest puppy attire**,
and set out to find a career.
Then **Bean** happened upon a **big house full of kids**
who all needed a good deal of **cheer.**

Then he thought, "This is where I can be a **good dog—**
make a **difference** instead of a **mess!**"
So he asked if they needed a **fun little pup,**
and, of course, the response was **"OH, YES!"**

So they named him **"Director of Love and Compassion,"**
and Bean did his new job with pride.

But one day, he decided that he'd **break a rule**
when a **child needed him** by her side.

Mr. Bean snuck upstairs and he promptly got **caught**—man, he thought he'd be **fired for sure!**

But the grown-ups said, "**NO!** We would hate you to **go...** you're the pup that we **love and adore!**

Now he's been here for years, through the **laughter and tears**
and he's loved by **the kids** in this place.

He breaks rules here and there, but folks don't seem to care once he gives them **a lick on the face.**

ABOUT
RONALD McDONALD HOUSE CHARITIES
of KANSAS CITY

· · · · · · · · · · · · · ·

Our mission is to reduce the burden of childhood illness on children and
their families. Throughout our three Houses and Family Room inside of
Children's Mercy Hospital, we provide a home away from home for families
with children who are receiving medical treatment in Kansas City-area hospitals.
We offer home-cooked meals, comfortable beds, hot showers, and a friendly,
loving environment for 87 families every night—so they can stay close to their
child to provide love and support throughout the healing process.

· · · · · · · · · · · · ·